Silas Weir Mitchell

Francis Drake: a tragedy of the sea

Silas Weir Mitchell

Francis Drake: a tragedy of the sea

ISBN/EAN: 9783743305304

Manufactured in Europe, USA, Canada, Australia, Japa

Cover: Foto ©Andreas Hilbeck / pixelio.de

Manufactured and distributed by brebook publishing software
(www.brebook.com)

Silas Weir Mitchell

Francis Drake: a tragedy of the sea

FRANCIS DRAKE

A Tragedy of the Sea

BY

S. WEIR MITCHELL, M. D., LL. D. Harv.

AUTHOR OF "A PSALM OF DEATHS," ETC.

BOSTON AND NEW YORK
HOUGHTON, MIFFLIN AND COMPANY
The Riverside Press, Cambridge
1893

The Riverside Press, Cambridge, Mass., U. S. A.
Electrotyped and Printed by H. O. Houghton & Co.

TO

M. C. M.

PREFACE

THE difficulty of realizing to-day the feelings and motives of the men of another era is well illustrated in the incidents on which I have based the dramatic poem of "Francis Drake." In the poetical telling of it I have adhered with reasonable fidelity to the somewhat varying statements given in "The World Encompassed" (1628), Hakluyt Society, No. 16; the extracts of evidence as to the trial of Doughty from the Harleian manuscripts, in the same volume; Barrow's life of Drake; and an admirable but brief biography of the great sea-captain by Julius Corbett, in English Men of Action. I have had neither desire nor intention to make of this strange story an acting drama. Doughty, as he is drawn by Mr. Corbett, must have been, as he says, an Iago of rare type. A scholar, a soldier, a gentleman of the Inner Temple, more or less learned in Hebrew, Greek, and Latin, he seems to have had great power to attract the affections of men. That he betrayed his friend's trust, and was guilty of mutiny, and even of contemplating darker crime, appears probable, although as to the details of this sad story we know little, but small fragments of the evidence given on the trial having been preserved. The historian, more than the poet, may well be perplexed at the nobler characteristics which appear in this singular being on the approach of death. It is here that the judgments of to-day fail us before the account of the quiet, cheerful talk[1] at dinner while the headsman waits. An immense curiosity fills us as to what was said. Then, there is the sacrament taken with Drake, the final embrace, the remarkable words of quotation from Sir Thomas More,[2] omitted in the play, and at last the axe and block.

---

[1] "They dined, also at the same table together, as cheerfully in sobriety as ever in their lives they had done aforetime; each cheering up the other, and, taking their leave, by drinking each to other, as if some journey only had been in hand." (*World Encompassed*, p. 67. Hakluyt Society's edition.)

[2] Doughty is credited in one account of his death with saying to the executioner, when about to lay his head on the block, "As good Sir Thomas More said, 'I fear thou wilt have little honesty [*i. e.* credit] of so short a neck.'"

Except as to one anachronism, which I leave
the critics to discover, the main events of this
dramatic tale are on the whole historically cor-
rect. It is likely that the part played in the
poem by the chaplain would be justified, had
we all the evidence. His disgrace later in the
voyage throws light upon his conduct at the
trial. It is worthy of note that there is no
woman in this tragic story.

BAR HARBOR, 1892.

FRANCIS DRAKE

A Tragedy of the Sea

Time, 1578.

Off the coast of Patagonia. On board the Pelican, the Elizabeth, and the Plymouth.

DRAMATIS PERSONÆ.

FRANCIS DRAKE, *Admiral.*

THOMAS DOUGHTY, *his friend, a gentleman venturer.*

FRANCIS FLETCHER, *Chaplain.*

JOHN WINTER,

LEONARD VICARY, } *Captains.*

WILLIAM CHESTER,

SEAMEN.

GENTLEMEN.

FRANCIS DRAKE

Deck of the Elizabeth. Fleet in the offing.

JOHN WINTER. THOMAS DOUGHTY.

Doughty (coming aboard). Good-morrow,
  Winter.   Still the winds are foul.
I would they blew from merry England shores.

  Winter. I would they had not blown you to
  my ship.
None are more welcome elsewhere.   Strict commands
Forbid this visiting from ship to ship.

  Doughty. These orders are most wise, — I
  doubt not that ;
Yet must I learn that any here afloat
Is master of the gentlemen who venture
Their ducats and their lives.   Let him make laws
To rule rough sailors ; they are not for us.

  Winter. Yet one must be the master.   Ill it
  were
If, drifting masterless, this little realm

Of tossing ships obeyed not one sure helm.
I shall best serve you if I bid you go.

    Doughty.   The Pelican is twice a league away.
'T is time the several captains of the fleet
Should learn how little mind the seamen have,
Ay, and the gentlemen, to hold our course.
Now, were we all of us of one firm mind,
This cheating voyage should end, and that full
    soon.
This in your ear.   Did I dare speak of Leices-
    ter —   [*Winter recoils.*

    Winter.   Have you a mind to lose us both
    our heads ?
I would not ill report you, but your words
Sail near to treason, both to Queen and friend.
I understand you not.

    Doughty.   Nor always I myself.
I pray you but this once be patient with me.
My actions shall not lack support in England.
If I might dare say all, you best of any
Would know the admiral has no better friend.
The ships decay ; the sailors mutiny ;
Before us lies a waste of unknown seas ;
Methinks authority doth beget in men
A certain madness.   Think you if we chance

To ruin peaceful towns and scuttle ships,
And rouse these Spanish hornets on their coasts,
Think you the dearest counsellor of the Queen —
I dare not name him — will be better pleased
With him that hurts or him that helps this
    voyage?

    Winter. I think your enterprise more peril-
    ous
Than half a hundred voyages, good friend, —
I pray you risk not losing of the name,
For you are greatly changed from him I knew
This some time past of gentle disposition;
In danger tranquil; gay, and yet discreet;
Learned in the law, a scholar and a soldier.

    Doughty. An old-time nursery trick: comfits
    before,
And after comes the dose; then sweets again.

    Winter. Be not so hasty; hear me to the end,
And be my careful friendship early pardoned.
I have heard you say of late you lack advance-
    ment.
There is advancement no man need to lack
Who makes his Duty like a mother's knees,
Where all his prayers are said. This man you
    were.

What other man is this I hardly know:
One that of all his natural endowments
Makes but base use to stir the meaner sort,
To darken counsel with a mist of words,
To scatter falsehood, and to sow distrust;
And all as lightly as a housewife flings
The morning grain amidst her cackling crew.

> *Doughty.* You have done well to ask my pardon first.

> *Winter.* Nay. I do hold the bond of friendship strong;

And he who wills to keep his friends must know
To stomach that they lack. I would indeed
You had not spoken as you have to-day.

> *Doughty.* What matters it? My words are safe with you.

> *Winter.* Safe as my countenance will let them be;

Safe till the admiral asks, and, like a boy,
I stand a-twiddliug of uneasy thumbs,
On this foot, now, or that, red in the face.
By Heaven! what fetched you on this hated voyage?

> *Doughty.* A trick. A fetch indeed!

> *Winter.*   Nay, that's not so.

Trick or no trick, this is not English earth,
Nor Drake the man who on the Devon greens
Sat half the night a-talking poesy.
I have seen many men in angry moods,
But this man's wrath is as the wrath of God,
Instant and terrible.   Pray you, be warned,
And if your soul be capable of fear —
    Doughty. Fear!
    Winter. Ay, a healthful virtue in its place.
Had I been but the half as rash as you,
My very sword would tremble in its sheath.
    Doughty. And yet I have no nearer friend
        than he.
    Winter. You judge men by their love, as
        maidens do.
    Doughty. And not an ill way, either, as earth
        goes.
The admiral in his less distracted times
Hath some rare flavour of the woman in him.
    Winter. Oh, that's the half of him : no lady
        wronged,
No pillaged church, no hurt of unarmed man,
Will stain his record at the great account.
Have then a care.   The gentle, just, and brave
Are ill to anger.

Doughty.   What I say to you
I not less easily shall say to him,
Trusting the friendly equity of his love.

Winter. A certain devil lurks in every angel,
Else had there never been a strife in heaven.
Now on my soul I wonder at the patience
Which thrice has warned you as a brother
        might,
And once removed you from a high command.
'T is very strange to me how men may differ.
No doubts have I; along these savage coasts
Magellan sailed.   Are we not English born ?

Doughty. I neither have forgotten nor forget.
Thanks for your patience.   There is more to
        say
That might be said.

Winter.   I would it had been less.
I think it well no other hears your words.

Doughty. Oh, fear not I shall rashly squan-
        der speech.

Winter. Spend not your thoughts at all. Be
        miserly.
These wooden walls have echoes ; to and fro
Some wild word wanders, till, on each return,
We less and less our own mind's children know.

All gold they say goes through the devil's mint;
But words are very devils of themselves.
I do commend you to a fast of speech.

    Doughty. It might be wise.

    Winter (*walks to the rail*). Come, let us
      shift the talk.

How huge and bloody red the moon to-night!
This utter quiet of the brooding sea
I like not overwell; nor yon red moon.
So, there 's a breeze again, and now 't is still.
We shall have storms to-morrow.

    Doughty.   More 's the reason,
Before our ships are scattered far and wide,
That I should speak what others dare not speak.

    Winter. I 'll hear no more. My mother used
      to say
That silence was a very Christian virtue.
When I talk folly, be the Moon my friend;
There are no eavesdroppers among the stars.

    Doughty. Her sex they say are leaky coun-
      sellors;
And, too, she shares thy secrets with a man,
Red i' the visage now. Here 's three to keep
Thy pleasant indiscretions.

    Winter.   Happy Moon!

That ere a day is dead shall England see.

Ah, gentle dame, shine on our island homes;

Kiss for my sake a face as fair as thine;

Go tell our love to every maiden flower

That droops tear-laden in our Devon woods.

    Doughty. I dreamed last night that never
       more again

Should I see England.

    Winter.   That 's as God may will.

    Doughty. God or the Devil!

    Winter.   Hush! When night is come,

And all the mighty spaces overhead

And all this vast of sea lie motionless,

God seems so near to me, ill deeds so far,

That all my soul in gentled wonder bides.

                      [*They are silent a time.*

    Doughty. Mark how the southward splendour
       of the cross

Shines peace upon us. When the nights are
       calm,

I joy to climb the topmast's utmost peak,

And, hanging breathless in the unpeopled void,

Note how the still deep answers star for star.

    Winter. See, the wind freshens. Get you to
       your ship.

Come not again.   This seeming quiet sea
Is not more dangerous than a man you know.
  Doughty. I shall not spare to think upon
     your words.
My thanks, and pleasant dreams.   Good-night.
  Winter. Good-night.

               [*Doughty goes to his boat.*

              Cabin of Pelican.

         DRAKE.   VICARY.   WINTER.

  Winter. It sorts not with my honour that I
     speak.
  Drake. Enough to know John Winter will
     not speak ;
A cruel verdict is the just man's silence.
I have been patient, but the end has come.
What breeds these discontents ?   I know the
     man.
Were he twin brother of my mother's womb
He should not live to mar my Prince's venture.
(*To Vicary.*) Are you struck silent, like my
     good John Winter ?
What substance is there in this mutinous talk ?

Vicary. Too little substance, not enough to
    eat ;
Too much of parson, and some empty bellies.
A very mutinous thing 's an empty paunch.
    Drake. Now here 's a man has never a plain
    answer.
Out with it in good English.
    Vicary.   As you will.
I pray you pardon me my way of speech ;
I cannot help it. I was born a-grinning,
Or so my mother said. If death 's a jest,
I doubt not I shall never die in earnest.
    Drake. Now on my soul this passes all en-
    durance ;
Grin, if it please you, but at least speak out.
    Vicary. I never had as little mind to speak.
    Drake. I have heard you jesting with a Span-
    ish Don
When sore beset and wellnigh spent with
    wounds.
I think some counsel lies behind your mirth.
    Vicary. Were I the admiral I would preach
    a sermon.
    Drake. A sermon !
    Vicary.   Yea ! and that a yardarm long,

With master parson for sole auditor.

Also good rum 's a very Christian diet,

And vastly does console a shrunken belly.

> *Drake (smiling).* Well, my gay jester, is
> there more to say ?

> *Vicary.* I have sometimes thought we carry
> on our ships

Too large a freight of time.

> *Drake.* Talk plain again.

It takes three questions to beget an answer.

> *Vicary.* Now, as the world runs, that 's un-
> natural many.

> *Drake.* I think you will not speak.

> *Vicary.* No, I 'm run dry.

I am as barren as a widowed hen.

> *Drake (laughing).* Out with you ! Go !

> *Vicary (aside).* And none more glad to go.
>> [*Exit Vicary.*

> *Drake.* One that must needs be taken in his
> humour.

> *Winter.* 'T is a strange disposition that hath
> mirth

For what breeds tears in others.

> *Drake.* No, not strange.

But I 've no jesting in my heart to-day.

The straits lie yonder, dark and perilous;
The Spaniards' villainies sit heavy here.

[Strikes his breast.

Their racks are red with honest English blood;
The dead call "Come." Ah, Winter, by my soul,
When Panama is ours, when their galleons lie
Distressful wrecks, and England's banner flies
Unquestioned on the far Pacific sea,
Then —

> *Winter.* Is it so? Runs your commission
> thus?

> *Drake.* Once past the straits, and all shall
> know my errand.

Here is the warrant of Her Majesty,
And here the sword she bade me call her own.

> *Winter.* Did Doughty know of this?

> *Drake.*   Ay, from the first.

> *Winter.* A double treason.

> *Drake.*   Counsel me, John Winter.

The sailors murmur, and the gentlemen
Sow quarrels and dissension through the fleet.
My dearest friend betrays my dearest trust.
What means this gay boy's chatter about time?

> *Winter.* A riddle easily read, if you but
> think

What use the devil has for idle hours.

Drake. I have long meant to make an end
 of that.
Go tell these lazy gentles Francis Drake
Bids them to haul and pull as sailors do;
Ay, let them reef and lay out on the yards.
I 'll bid 'gainst Satan for their idleness.
Belike they may not care to go aloft;
Then, on my word, I 've bilboes down alow.
 Winter. Thou wouldst not set a gentleman
  i' the stocks?
 Drake. Parson or gentle, let them try me
  not.
'T is said a gibbet stands on yonder shore:
There brave Magellan hanged a mutinous Don.
Let them look to it. See I be obeyed.
None shall be favoured. Fetch me now aboard
This traitor Doughty, and no words with him.
 Winter. Ay, ay, sir.
 Drake.   Go. Let there be no delay.
    [*Winter in his boat beside the Plymouth.*
Doughty (*descending*). What means this
 summons?
 Winter.   Hush! I may not speak.
Give way there, men. (*To Doughty.*) Have
 you your tablets with you?
     [*Takes them and writes.*

"Take care. Be warned. The devil is broke
    loose."

Doughty.   Is it so? Why am I bidden?

Winter.   Way there, men!

Doughty.   Will you not answer me?

Winter.   Not I, indeed.
Way there, enough! Ho, there, aboard!

>   [*Doughty goes aboard the Pelican.*

Doughty.   Good-night.

Deck of Pelican.

DOUGHTY. FLETCHER.

Fletcher.   I think there is some mischief in
    the air.
'T is said the admiral has sent for you.

Doughty.   I'm haled aboard with no more
    courtesy
Than any meanest ruffian of the crew.
Were I in England he should answer me.

Fletcher.   This is not England.

Doughty.   Oh, by heaven! no!
(*Aside.*) Time must be won. I've been a loi-
    tering fool.
(*Aloud.*) I would that I could clear my mind
    to you.

Fletcher. Why not to me? What other is
  so fit?
Is not confession like an act of nature?
  Doughty. I am like a wine thick with con-
    fusing lees.
To-day they settle, and to-morrow morn
Another shakes me, and I 'm thick again.
  [*Fletcher watches him. Both are silent for a moment.*
Thou art both man and priest.
  Fletcher.   Add friend to both.
  Doughty. You said, most reverend sir, both
    man and priest.
Had you been more of man, yet all of priest,
Confession had been easier.
  Fletcher.   More of man!
Grant you I lack the courage of the sea,
Think you it takes none to be now your friend?
I have the will, ay, and the resolution,
To help you where I think you most need help.
I guess the half your lips delay to tell.
  Doughty (looking about him). Enough.
    Time passes, and you should know all.
My Lord of Burleigh much mislikes this voy-
  age.
Who helps to ruin it will no loser be.

Had I but known this ere my florins went
To aid a foolish venture !

 Fletcher.   But the Queen —

 Doughty. Hath ever had two minds, as is her
  way.

(*Points north.*) Now there advancement lies.
  (*Points south.*) And that way death.

 Fletcher. Thou art in the service of my Lord
  of Burleigh ?

Not more than thou am I the admiral's man.

 Doughty. And I am no man's man ; I am
  the Queen's.

I shall best serve my God in serving her.

Shall it be Prince or friend ? I may not both.

 Fletcher. Is he thy friend ?

 Doughty.   Of late I doubt it much.

Now hath he closer counsellors than I.

 Fletcher. He loves thee not. This ill-ad-
  visèd voyage

Goes to disaster in these unknown seas

Where some foul devil led the sons of Rome.

I have heard that demons lit them down the
  coast.

This nine and fifty years no Christian sail

Has gone this deathful way. The admiral

Knows not the sullen temper of the fleet.

(*Looks at Doughty steadily.*) There should be
    one — a friend — to bid him turn

And set our prows toward England.   Think
    upon it.

Doughty. But who shall bell the cat? What
    mouse among us ?

Fletcher. If but we English mice were of
    one mind !

Doughty. Soon shall we be so.   You have
    unawares

Made firm my purpose.   'T is not in thy kind

To court such peril as our talk may bring.

The more for this have you my thanks.
    Enough.

The counsel you have given —

Fletcher (*alarmed*).   I gave you none.

Doughty. Oh, rest you easy.   It is safe with
    me.

As you are priest, so I am gentleman ;

Now in the end it comes to much the same.

Enter CHESTER.

Chester (*to Doughty*).   The admiral would
    see you instantly.   [*Exit.*

Cabin of Pelican.

Drake. I could wish this man had been less
    dear to me.
Another I had long since crushed.   The rat
Which gnaws the planks between our lives and
    death
I had as lightly dealt with.   For love's sake
And all the honest past that has been ours
Once shall I speak.   Ay, once!   [*A knock.*
                    Ho, there.   Come in.

Enter CHESTER *and* DOUGHTY.

Chester. The land lies low to westward, and
    the wind
Blows fair and steady.   [*Drake looks at the chart.*
Drake.   Ay, St. Julian's isle.
                            [*Exit Chester.*
(*To Doughty.*) Pray you be seated.
    Doughty.   I am ordered hither.
'T were fit I stand.
    Drake.   Yes, I am admiral ;
But there are moments in the lives of all
When the stern conscience of a too great office
Appals the kindlier heart that fain would be

Where indecisions breed less consequence.

I said, be seated.   [*Doughty obeys.*

Are you not my friend?

Forget these rolling seas, the time, the place,

This mighty errand which my Prince has sped.

Think me to-day but simple Francis Drake,

And be yourself the brother of my heart.

    Doughty. There spoke the old Frank Drake
        I seemed to lose.

    Drake. Let us try back. We are like ill-
        broken dogs.

Our lives have lost the scent.

    Doughty.   Nay, think not so.

    Drake. Ah, once I had a friend, a scholar
        wise,

A soldier, and a poet; dowered, I think,

With all the gentle gifts that win men's hearts.

Of late he seems another than himself;

Of late he is most changed, and him I knew

Is here no more.   Ah, but I too am double,

And one of me is still thy nearest friend,

And one, ah, one is admiral of the fleet.

Let him that loves you whisper to your soul

The thing he would not say.   You understand.

Ah, now you smile.   A pretty turn of phrase

Did ever capture you.   'T was always thus.
We have seen death so often, eye to eye,
That fear of death were idle argument;
Yet in such words of yours as men report
A deathful sentence lurks.   Oh, cast away
These mad temptations, won I know not whence.
Last night I fell to thinking, ere I slept,
Of those proud histories of older days
You loved to tell amid the tents in Ireland.
Trust me, no one of these that shall not fade
Before the wonder of this English tale
Of what El Draco and his captains did.
And when, at twilight, by our Devon hearths
Some old man tells the story, shall he pause,
And say, But one there was, of England born,
That sowed the way with perils not of God,
Breeding dissension, casting on his name
Dishonour —

    Doughty (leaping up).   Now, by heaven! no
       man shall say —
    *Drake (smiling and quiet, puts a hand on
       each shoulder of Doughty).*   Hush! you
       will waken up that other man.

Read not my meaning wrong.   I am sore beset.
Before me lie dark days.   The timid shrink;

The gentlemen, who should have been my stay,
Fall from me useless. Yet, come what come
    may,
For England's glory and my lady's grace,
I go my way. Well did he speak who said,
" Heaven is as near by water as by land."
And therefore, whether it be death or fame
That waits in yonder seas, I go my way.
Yet, if I lose you on this venturous road,
Half the proud joy of victory were gone.
I have been long ; you, patient.   Rest we here.
    Doughty.   Yes, I am more than one man ;
      more 's the pity.
If I have sinned, forgive me, and good-night.
    Drake. Thou shalt stay with me on the Pel-
      ican.
    Doughty (aside). So, so. A child in ward !
    (Aloud.) Again, good-night.   *[Exit.*

          Enter VICARY.

Vicary. The water shoals. A land lies west
    by south.
There seems good anchorage in the island's lee.
    Drake. We shall find water here, good fruit
    and fish.

Send in a boat for soundings. Signal all
To anchor where seems best ; and Vicary,
Set thy gay humour to some thoughtful care
Of him that left just now. I hold him dear.

> *Vicary.* I would to heaven he were safe in
> England.

> *Drake.* And I, and I. He is more like a
> child

Than any man my life's experience knows.
Yet he is dangerous to himself and us:
Too fond of speech; too cunning with the
> tongue,
That tempts to mischief like a sharpened blade.

> *Vicary.* Ah, words! words! words! Ye
> children of the fiend,

On all your generated repetitions
Are visited your parents' wickedness.
He keeps boon company with each man's hu-
> mour,
Is gay with me, is chivalrous with you,
At Winter's side a grave philosopher.
I shall set merry sentinels for his guards,
And there my wisdom ends.

> *Drake.*   My thanks. No more.
> > [*Exit Vicary.*

Deck of Pelican. Ships at anchor near the north end of the island.

DOUGHTY. WINTER. SEAMEN.

Winter. These are my orders.

Doughty.   I may not to shore,
And for the reason ?   Drake shall give it me.
(*Turns to the men.*) I hear there is no water
    on these shores.

1st Sailor. That in the casks is but mere
mud of vileness ; rot in the mouth, and stenches
in the nose.

2d Sailor. And for the biscuits, they are
mouldy green, and inhabited like an owl's nest
with all manner of live things.

3d Sailor. It will be worse in the lower seas.
There the men are eleven cubits tall.

2d Sailor. Nay, feet, and that 's enough.

4th Sailor. Where scurvy Dons have gone,
good English may.

Doughty. We gentles are no better off than
    you.
Here is an order we shall pull and haul,
And lay aloft.   What !   Lack ye meat to-day ?

Here are grubs to spare. These caverned bis-
    cuits hold
Small beeves in plenty. Here 's more life, I
    think,
Than we are like to find on yonder coast.

1st Sailor. A Portugee did tell me once
there was no day in the straits where we must
sail, and all the sea be full of venomed snakes.

Doughty. Nay. That 's a foolish fable.
True it is that in the straits are mighty isles of
ice, with sail and mast. They beat about, men
say, like luggers on a wind, and never man to
handle rope or sail.

Fletcher. The boats are come again, and no
water, none! Alas, this miserable voyage!

        Enter VICARY *from boat.*

Vicary. Not so, good chaplain. Underneath
    a cliff
I found a spring as sweet as England's best.
Good store of shellfish too, and these strange
    fruits.
(*To Doughty.*) You 're but an old-wife at
these fireside tales. Lord, lads! there 's won-
ders yonder. It is twice as good as a fair in

May. There is a merry-go-round that 's called a swirlpool. Round you go, a hundred years, ship and all, not a farthing to pay, and then home to bed, with addled pates, as good as drunk, and no man the poorer. [*The men laugh.*

1st Sailor (aside). He do lie to beat a rusty weathercock.

2d Sailor. But men do say there 's hell-traps set along the rocks, and all the waters boil like witch's pots.

Vicary (laughs). The tale is gone awry. When last I sailed this way, no fire would burn, and all the little fiends were harvesting of mighty icicles to keep the daddy devils from frosted toes.

1st Sailor (aside). He be a lively liar. He be a very flea among liars. [*All laugh.*

Vicary. The seas be rum, and all the whales mad drunk. [*Laughter.*
I thought my laughter trap was baited well.

4th Sailor (aside). He don't starve his lies. A very pretty liar. His lies be fat as ever a Christmas hog.

Vicary. Tom Doughty, I 'll match lies with you, my lad,
The longest day of June. A song, a song!

Sailors. A song, a song! The captain for
a song!
That song the captain made the day we sailed
From Cadiz road, and left their fleet ablaze.
Vicary. Here 's for a song. The admiral
bids say
Your rum is doubled for a week to come.
So here we go. Be hearty with the burden.

SONG.

Queen Bess has three bad boys,
        Such naughty boys!
They sailed away to Cadiz bay
To make a mighty noise.
        Heave her round!
        Heave her round!
            Such bad boys!
            Yo ho!

There 's wicked Master Drake,
As likes to play with guns ;
He sailed away to Cadiz bay
To wake the sleepy Dons.
        Heave her round! etc.

These be three captains small,
None taller than a splinter.
One does admire to play with fire,
That 's little Jacky Winter.
          Heave her round! etc.

There 's one does love to fight,
It might be Billy Chester.
And they 're away to Cadiz bay
Before a stiff sou'-wester.
          Heave her round! etc.

Don Spaniard sings, Avast!
What 's doing with them grapples?
We 're just Queen Bess's naughty boys,
We 're only stealing apples.
          Heave her round! etc.

They filled their little stomachs,
They had a pretty frolic.
The boys as ate the apples up
Was n't them as had the colic.
          Heave her round! etc.

Small Frank, he shot his gun,
And Willy played with fire.

To see those naughty boys again
No Spaniard do desire.

> Heave her round ! etc.

Vicary. Well tuned, my lads. Now who of
> you 's for shore?

Doughty (aside to a mate). There 'll be no
> songs down yonder.

Winter (leaning over him). What, again?
More mischief, ever more? Dark is the sea
Where you will sail. What fiend possesses you?
This in your ear. The priest is no man's friend.
If I do know the malady of baseness,
There 's one that needs a doctor.

Doughty. You are wrong.
I have no better friend, none more assured.

> *Winter.* Indeed, I think you are too rich in
> friends.

Better you had a hundred eager foes
Than this man's friendly company. One step
> more,
One slight excess of speech, some word retold, —
And thou art lost to life.

Doughty. He dare not do it!

Winter. Dare not! I think it oft doth
> chance a man

Knows not his nearest friend as others do.

As for thy priest, — I greatly fear a coward.

The day will come when honest Francis Drake

Will shake all secrets from him as a dog

Shakes out a rat's mean life.   Beware the day !

Well do I know the admiral's silent mood ;

Then should men fear him, and none more than
    you,

Because he dreads the counsel of his heart.

[Exit both.

*Deck of the Pelican.   Evening, a week later.   The
    fleet at anchor near the south end of the island
    of St. Julian.   Sailors at the capstan.*

Winter. Now, then, to warp her in.   Round
    with the capstan.

Sailors and gentlemen, bear all a hand !

Doughty. Not I, by heaven ! Not I ! My
    father's son

Stains not his sword-hand with this peasant toil.

Gentlemen. Nor I ! nor I ! nay, never one
    of us.

Winter. Do as I bid you !

Doughty.   Not a band of mine

Shall to this sailor work.

Winter.   That shall we see.

[*Walks to the cabin. Boatswain whistles. Men man the capstan, singing.*

Yo ho! Heave ho!
Oh, it 's ingots and doubloons,
Oh, it 's diamonds big as moons,
     As we sail,
     As we sail.
Yo ho! Heave ho!

Oh, it 's rusty, crusty Dons,
And it 's rubies big as suns,
     As we sail, etc.

Oh, it 's pieces by the scores,
And it 's jolly red moidores,
     As we sail, etc.

Oh, we 'll singe King Philip's beard,
And no man here afeard,
     As we sail, etc.

Enter VICARY.

Vicary. Well sung. Well hauled, my lads.
(*To Doughty.*) A word with you.

You will attend the admiral in his cabin.

(*Aside to Doughty.*) Ware cat, good mouse!
The claws are out to-night!

Doughty. 'T were better soon than later.
After you.   [*Exit.*

Cabin of Pelican.

DRAKE. WINTER.

Enter VICARY, *followed by* DOUGHTY.

Drake. Pray you be seated. (*To Doughty.*)
Nay, not you, not you.

(*To Winter.*) Arrest this gentleman.

Winter.   Your sword, an 't please you.
                                        [*Receives it.*

Drake. I charge you here with treason to
the Queen.

You shall to trial with no long delay.

Doughty. What court is this with which you
threaten me?

Drake. Now, by St. George, your lawyer
tricks and quibbles

Shall help you little. I am Francis Drake,
The Queen's plain sailor, and the master here.

Doughty. Master!

Drake. Ay, master! Traitor to the Queen,
This long account is closed. All, all is known,
Since when, at Plymouth, on the eve we sailed,
My Lord of Burleigh bought you; what the
    price,
The devil knows — and you.
    Doughty.   My Lord of Burleigh!
I pray you speak of this with me alone.
What I would say is for a secret ear.
    Drake. No, by my sword, not I!
    Doughty.   Then have thy way.
No law can touch me here. This is not Eng-
    land.
    Drake. Where sails a plank in English for-
    ests hewn,
There England is. This deck is England now,
And I a sea-king of this much of England.
Put me this man in irons! See to it!
Let him have speech of none except yourselves.
                [*Exit Winter and Doughty.*
(*To Vicary.*) I have too long delayed.
    Vicary.   That may well be.
    Drake. I hear he hath great favour with the
    crews,
A maker of more mischief than I guessed.

Vicary. Men love him well.

Drake.   He hath too many friends.
This is the very harlotry of friendship.
Go now, and pray that when command is yours
You have no friends. See that strict guard be
            kept.   [*Exit Vicary.*
(*Alone.*) I would that God had spared me
      this one hour.

Pelican. DOUGHTY *in irons on the deck, seated upon
      a coil of ropes, leaning against a mast.*

Winter (to the guards). Back there, my
      men !

Doughty. You are most welcome, Winter.
I am very glad of company. My soul
Is sick to surfeit of its own dull thoughts.
I like not lonely hours. What land is that ?

Winter. St. Julian's cape.

Doughty.   Is that a cross I see ?
It seems, I think, the handiwork of man.

Winter. No cross is that ; there stout Magel-
      lan hanged
Don Carthagene, vice-admiral of his fleet.

Doughty.   Wherefore ?

Winter.   'T is said he did dislike the voyage,
And had no mind to pass the narrow straits.

   Doughty.   The strait he chose was narrower;
     mayhap
He had no choice — as I may not to-morrow.

                        [*Is silent a few moments.*

A little while ago, the scent of flowers
Came from the land.   Their nimble fragrance
   woke,
As by a charm, some sleeping memories.
I dreamed myself again a fair-haired boy,
A-gathering cowslips in my mother's fields.

                             [*Pauses.*

There is no order that I shall not sing;
I can no mighty treason set to song.

   Winter.   Sing, if it please you.   I 'll be glad
     it doth.
What song shall 't be?

   Doughty.   Ah me, those Devon lanes!

                            [*Sings.*

SONG.

I would I were an English rose,
  In England for to be;
The sweetest maid that Devon knows
  Should pick, and carry me.

To pluck my leaves be tender quick,
A fortune fair to prove,
And count in love's arithmetic
Thy pretty sum of love.

[*The men come nearer.*

Oh, Devon's lanes be green o'ergrown,
And blithe her maidens be,
But there be some that walk alone,
And look across the sea.

1st *Sailor.*　'T is a sad shame so gay a gentleman
Should lie in irons.

2d *Sailor.*　　　　Ay, the pity of it.

Winter (to the men). Off with you there!
(*To Doughty.*) The devil's in your
tongue!
Why must you sing of England? Follow me.
I think you would breed mutiny in heaven.

[*Exit.*

Cabin of Pelican.

DRAKE. *Enter* FLETCHER.

Fletcher. I am come as bidden. What may
be your will?

Drake. Think you a man may serve two masters?

Fletcher.   Nay,
'T is not so writ.
    Drake.   Yet there are some I know
Would have me serve a dozen, and my Queen.
Shall I serve this man's doubt, and that man's
    fear?
Who bade these cowards follow me to sea?
And you, that are Christ's captain,—what of
    you?
Were I a man vowed wholly unto God,
I should have courage both of God and man;
And fear 's a malady of swift infection.
    Fletcher. I think my captain has been ill in-
    formed.
    Drake. Ah, not so ill. Look at me, in the
    face;
A man's eyes may rest honest, though his soul
Be deeper damned than Judas. Thou art false!
False to thy faith, thy duty, and thy Prince!
Now, if thou hast no righteous fear of God —
By heaven! here stands a man you well may fear.
    Fletcher. Indeed I know not how I 've an-
    gered you.
    Drake. Thou shalt know soon. And — look
    not yet away —

You have hatched treason with the larger help
Of one that hath more courage. Spare him
    not
If you have hope to see another day.
What of your plans? I charge you, sir, be
    frank.
What has he told that you should fear to tell?
    Fletcher. We did but talk. Haply I may
    have said
I do not love the sea, that some aboard
Would be well pleased to stand on English soil.
    Drake. If you have any wisdom of this
    world,
A coward heart may save a foolish head.
I asked you what this coward Doughty said ;
You answer me with babble of yourself.
Speak out, or, by my honour, — no light oath, —
I shall so score you with the boatswain's lash
That Joseph's coat shall be a mock to yours.
    Fletcher. You would not — dare —
    Drake.   I think you know me not.
You have my orders. Is it yes, or no ?
    Fletcher. I pray you, sir, consider what you
    ask.
No priest of God may, without deadly sin,

Speak what in penitence a troubled soul
Has in confession whispered.   Ask me not.

Drake. If I do understand your words aright,
Save for the idle talk of idle men,
He hath said nought to you except of sin
Such as the best may in an hour of shame
Tell for the soul's relief.   If this be so,
Nor I, nor any man, may question you.

Fletcher. I do assure you that I spoke the
truth.

Drake (perplexed, walks to and fro. Turns
suddenly, offering the hilt of his sword).
Swear it upon the cross-hilt of my sword.
Swear !   [*Fletcher hesitates.*

As my God is dear, thou art more false
Than hell's worst devil.   Ho ! Without there !
Ho !

Fletcher. Nay, I will swear.

Drake.   Too late.   Without there ! Ho !
Send me the boatswain's mate.   Without there !
Ho !
If I confess thee not, thou lying priest,
May I die old, — die quiet in my bed.
Ho there !   And quick !

Fletcher.   I pray you — let me think.

It may be that I did not understand.

It might be that he talked to me, a man,

As man to man. I think 't was even so.

    Drake. Out with it — quickly! Speak! Out!
        Out with it!

    Fletcher. I think he said the purpose of this
        voyage

Was hid, and all of us are cheated men.

It seems he said that if the gentles here

Were of one mind, and stirred the crews to act,

We might see England and our homes again.

    Drake. What more?

    Fletcher.   As who should take to bell the cat

As that the Queen your errand did not guess.

    Drake. So! Said he that? Go on; thy
        tale lacks wit.

    Fletcher. Also, that storms and vexing winds
        and currents

Did show God's will.

    Drake.   I think you trifle with me.

Did he talk ever of my Lord of Burleigh?

    Fletcher. I fear to speak.

    Drake.   Fear rather to be silent.

Here lies the warrant of her Majesty:

'T is she, not I, commands.

Fletcher.　　　　　　　　He seemed to say

They would best serve my Lord of Burleigh's
　　　wish

Who marred this venture, ere the power of
　　　Spain

Was roused to open war. I can no more.

　　Drake. See that your memory fail not on the
　　　morrow !

Go thank the devil in your prayers to-night

For that your skin is whole. Begone ! Begone !

　　　　　　　　　　　　　　[*Exit Fletcher.*

Now know I what it costs a woman-prince

To keep her realm. The great should have no
　　　friends.

　　Enter VICARY, WINTER, *and* CHESTER.

Drake. Call all the captains and the officers.

The court shall meet to-morrow morn, at eight.

There shall be charges ready in due form ;

You, all of you, shall hear the witnesses.

And, Winter, — we are far from England now, —

See that this trial be in all things fair,

As though each man of you, an ermined judge,

Sat in Westminster. Let no words of mine

Disturb the equities of patient judgment.

I would not that, when you and I are old,
Uneasy memories of too hasty action
Should haunt us with reproach.   But have a
    care.
My duty knows no friend ; be thine as ignorant.
Our fortunes and the honour of the Queen —
I should have said her honour and our for-
    tunes —
Rest in your hands.   See that my words be
    known.

Winter.   To all ?

Drake.   To all, sailors and gentlemen.
                              [*Exit the captains.*

WINTER, VICARY, *and* CHESTER *without.*

Chester.   I 'm like a child that fain would
    run away
To 'scape a whipping.

Winter.   There are none of us
More sore at heart than Drake.

Vicary.   I know of one.
I would a friend were dead ere break of day,
And all to-morrow's story left untold.
I think that I shall never laugh again.
                              [*They reach the deck.*

Chester (*pointing to the gibbet on the shore*).
    It may be yon long-memoried counsellor
Made hard the admiral's heart.

Vicary.   That might be so.
I wandered thither, yesterday, at eve,
And found a skull. Didst ever notice, Winter,
How this least mortal relic of a man
Does seem to smile? Hast ever talked with skulls?
They are courteous ever, and good listeners.
And never one of them, or man or maid,
That is not secret. There 's another virtue;
For what more honest and more chaste than death?
Now, then, this skull, that grins an hundred years, —
Pray think how mighty must the jest have been;
And then, how transient are our living smiles.

    Winter. Ill-omened talk. A graver business waits.

    Vicary. Give me an hour. I am not well to-day.
I will be with you very presently. [*Exit Vicary.*

*Evening of the day of the trial and condemnation
   of* DOUGHTY. *Time, sunset. Ashore on St. Julian's Island.*

WINTER. VICARY. DRAKE.

DRAKE *walking to and fro under the trees.*

Winter (coming up and walking beside him).
   What orders are there ?
Drake.   See the prisoner,
And bid him choose the hour and the day.
   Winter. And for the manner of the execu-
      tion ?
The court said nothing ; sir, it lies with you.
What is your pleasure ?
Drake.   Say my will, John Winter.
The gallows and the rope !
   Vicary (approaching).   Must it be so ?
That is a dog's death, not a gentleman's.
   Drake. I have at home a very honest dog.
   Vicary. Wilt pardon me if once again I
      plead ?
   Drake. Plead not with me.   No plea the
      heart can bring
My own heart fails to urge.

Winter.   I made no plea.
The man I loved, this morn for me was dead.
But there are those in England — far away —
Mother and sister —
  Drake.   Sir, you have my orders !
Henceforth no friends for me ! This traitor dies,
As traitors all should die, a traitor's death.
The man's life judges him, not you, nor I.
  Vicary. Indeed, the manner of a man's de-
      parture,
Whether upon a war-horse or an ass,
Doth little matter, as it seems to me,
If those he leaves feel not the fashion of it.
Now, many a year that rope will throttle me,
Who am no traitor, and who like not well
What treachery this man's nature moved him to.
  Drake. It seems to me that good men's lives
      are spent
In paying debts another makes for them.
I have my share. Take you your portion, too.
Be just, I pray you, both to him and me.
Now, here 's a man that was my closest friend.
In Plymouth, ay, in London, ere we sailed,
Against the pledge myself had given the Queen,
He told the purpose of my voyage to Burleigh,

Pledging himself to wreck this enterprise,
Lest we should rouse these Spanish curs to bite.
That I do hold the warrant of the Queen
Only this traitor knew, and, knowing it,
Has set himself to brewing discontent,
Stirred mutiny amidst my crews, cast wide
The seed of discord, till obedience,
That is the feather on the shaft of duty,
Failed, and my very captains questioned me.
One man must die, or this great venture dies ;
This man must die, or we go backward home,
Like mongrel dogs that fear a shaken stick.

 Winter. Yet none of us have asked his life
   of you.

 Drake. I ask it of myself ; shall ask it, sir,
Knowing how vain and pitiful my plea.
I have said nothing of the darker charge,
The covert hints, the whispering here and there
Of how my death might please my Lord of Bur-
   leigh,
And settle all these mutinous debates.
I think 't was but an idle use of speech ;
I think he meant not it should come to aught.

 Winter. Nor I.

 Vicary. Nor I. He hath confessed to all
Except this single charge. That he denied.

Drake. And now no more! And hope not I
    shall change.
Yet will I well consider all your words.
Rest you assured if there be any way
That both secures the safety of this voyage
And leaves this man to future punishment,
I shall not miss to find it.

Winter.   That were well.
I somewhat fear the temper of the men.
And these grave statesmen, closeted at home,
Have slight indulgence for the sterner needs
That whip us into what seems rash or cruel.

Drake. Ah, many a day 'twixt us and Eng-
    land lies,
And the peacemaker's blessing rests on time.
If death await me in the distant seas,
I shall not fear to meet a higher Judge.
If fortune smile upon our happy voyage,
No man in England that will dare to say
I served not well my country and my God;
The Queen will guard my honour as her own.
But, come what may, sirs, I shall act unmoved
By any dread of what the great may do,
Though we should prick this sullen Spain to
    war.

Vicary. Now, by St. George, could we but
    stir the Dons
To open fight! The Queen has many minds,
But when the blades are out, and Philip strikes,
As strike he will, these wary counsellors
Will lose her ear amid the clash of swords.
    Drake. Pray God that I do live to see the
    day
When all the might of England takes the sea,
And we, that are the falcons of the deep,
Shall tear these cruel vultures, till our beaks
Drip red with Spanish blood!
    Vicary.   May I be there!
    Drake (gravely). Trust me, we all shall live
    to see that hour.
God gives us moments when the years to come
Lie easily open like a much-read book.
Oppressed with weight of care, in these last
    days
I have seemed to see beyond this bitter time.
We shall so carry us in yon Rome-locked seas
That all the heart of England shall be glad,
And the brown mothers of these priest-led Dons
Shall scare unruly children with my name.
And then, and then, I see a nobler hour,

A day of mightier battle, when their fleets
Shall fly in terror from our English guns,
And through the long hereafter we shall sail
Unquestioned lords of all the watery waste.
Oh, 't was a noble dream!

Vicary.　　　　　　　　But what were life
Without the splendid prophecy of dreams?

　Drake.　At least, a moment they have given
　　release
From sadder thoughts of that which has to be.
The night is falling.　Get we now aboard.
To-morrow you shall have my final judgment.

*A cabin in the Pelican.　Early morning.　The day
　after the trial and condemnation of* DOUGHTY.

DOUGHTY.　*Enter* WINTER.

　Doughty.　Is there an hour set?　When shall
　　it be?

　Winter.　That rests with you.　Alas, too well
　　you know
That, being charged with certain grave offences,
Of which, to our great grief, you are not cleared,
The court decreed your death.　Now, I am come
To offer you thus much of grace —

Doughty.   As what?

Winter. Either to be at morning left ashore,
Or to be held till, at convenient time,
A ship may carry you to England, there
To answer for your deeds the Lords in Council;
Or will you take to be here done to death
As runs our sentence?

Doughty.   Would I had no choice.
That's a strange riddle! Here be caskets
    three.
'T is like the story in the Venice tale.
Thank Francis Drake for me. I 'll think
    upon it.
And send me Leonard Vicary with good speed.

  Winter. Is there aught else a man may do
    for you?

  Doughty. Yes, come no more until I send for
    you.

  Winter. Have I in anything offended you?

  Doughty. No, thou hast too much loved me;
    that is all.
The sting lies there.

  Winter.   I do not understand.

  Doughty. And I too well. Wilt send me
    Vicary?

Winter (*aside*). As strange a monitor for a
    mortal hour
As e'er a sick life's fancy hit upon.   [*Exit.*
    Doughty (*alone*). This is a sad disguise of
    clemency.
Death seemed a natural and a safe conclusion.
As one serenely bound upon a voyage,
I had turned my back on all I did hold dear,
And looked no more to land.   I think, indeed,
Almost the very touch and sound of life
Seemed fading, as when sleep comes whole-
    somely.
Now I am in the wakened world again,
And all the blissful company of youth,
Love, friendship, hope, the mere esteem of men,
Beckon, and mock me like to sunlit fields
Seen from the wave-crests where a swimmer
    strives,
Struck hither, thither, by uneasy seas.
Christ to my help!   Ah, counsel always best.

How should I bide upon these heathen shores?
Knowing how frail I be, how strong a thing
Is the contagion of base men's customs.
Alas! alas! I ever have been one

That wore the colour of the hour's friend.
What! risk my soul, that hath an endless date,
For days or years of life? That may not be.

What! home to England? I, a tainted man;
That's the gold casket where temptation lies.
There is no unconsidered blade of grass,
No little daisy, and no violet brief,
That does not hurt me with its sweet appeal.

                      [Walks to and fro.

I mind me of an evening — O my God!
No! That way anguish waits. I'll none of
    that.
Twice, in my dreams last night, I saw her come;
And twice she cried, "*First honour, and then
    love!*"
And came no more. O Jesu, hear my prayer,
And let me never in that other world
Meet the sad verdict of those troubled eyes
I kissed to tears the day we sailed away.

            Enter VICARY.

You are most welcome; sit beside me here.
I have found my sentence in a woman's eyes.
    Vicary. I understand.

Doughty.   How ever apt you are!
That took my fancy always.   Now, it saves
The turning of a dagger in a wound.
I have chosen death.
    Vicary.   And chosen well, I think.
There was not one of us that said not so;
Not one but wishes life were possible.
    Doughty. Set that aside.   It is not possi-
      ble.
And put no strain upon your natural self
To be another than the man you are.
Do you remember once a thing you said, —
How for the wise the soul has chapels four?
One, that I name not.   One, a home of tears.
One, the grave shrine of high philosophy.
And one, where all the saints are jesters gay.
Smile on me when I die.   In that dim world
I am assured men laugh, as well they may,
To see this ant-heap stirred.   Oh, I shall look
To see you smile.
    Vicary.   I pray you talk not thus.
    Doughty. And wherefore not?   A moment,
      only one,
The thought of England troubled my decision;
But that is over.   Yet, a word of home.

There is a maid in Devon — (*Hesitates.*) Par-
    don me.
When, by God's grace, you see her, as you must,
Tell her I loved her well, — and what beside
I leave to you.   I shall not hear the tale.
Be gentle in the way of your report.
Ah me! by every cross a woman kneels;
I doubt not, Leonard, that some Syrian girl
Sobbed where the thief hung dying.   Now,
    good-by!
Go! and remember — I shall hold you to it.
                        [*Exit Vicary.*

Oft when the tides of life were at their full,
I have sat wondering what the ebb would be,
And what that tideless moment men call death.
I think it strange as nears the coming hour,
I willingly would fetch it yet more near.
   Vicary (*without, as he goes on deck*).   He
    asks a smile where nature proffers tears.
I have laughed tears before, and may again.
Here dies a man who, like that heir of Lynne,
Has madly squandered honour, friendship, love,
And hath no refuge save the dismal rope.
Shall that bring other fortunes than he spent?
Ah me! I loved him well, — and I must smile; —

That will seem strange to men. I sometimes
    wish
I could feel sure that Christ did ever smile.

Enter DRAKE.

Drake. I come to hear thy choice.
Doughty.   My choice is made.
Death, and no long delay.   And be not troubled;
You will — ah, well I know you — feel the hurt.
Were you to say, " Take life, take hope again,
Take back command," and bid me mend my
    ways,
The mercy were but vanity of kindness.
Never could I be other than I am;
Yet think of me as but the minute's traitor.
You have been merciful.   'T is I am stern.
Not you, but I, decree that I shall die.
A sudden weariness of life is mine;
Let me depart in peace —
Drake.   Must it be so?
Another court may clear you.
Doughty.   Urge me not.
Another court!   There is but one high court
May clear my soul of guilt.   I go to God.
There shall be witnesses you may not call.

Let this suffice.   No man can move me now;
And rest assured I never loved you more.
   Drake. I thank you.   Now, what else?
   Doughty.   I choose to die.
Go we ashore at noon, and eat at table,
Like gentlemen who speed a parting friend
Upon a pleasant and a certain voyage.
And I would share with you the bread of God.
                               [*Pauses.*

There is one thing more, but one!
   Drake.   Speak!   Oh, my God!
Except — except mere life, there is no thing
I would not give you; yea, to my own life.
   Doughty. You cannot think that I would
      ask my life?
   Drake. Pardon, sweet gentleman, and sweeter
      friend.
   Doughty. There is a maid in Devon — Oh,
      Frank Drake!
It must not be the gibbet and the rope!
The axe and block, men say, cure all disgrace.
   Drake. So shall it be.
   Doughty.   I knew you not unkind.
I pray you leave me now.   God prosper you.
You cannot know how kind a thing is death.

*Island of St. Julian.   Table spread at noon, under
the trees.   DRAKE seated with DOUGHTY and
other officers.   In the background, a block, with
the headsman, sailors, and others.*

VICARY *and* WINTER *approach the table.*

Vicary. Didst hear, John Winter, what he
said to him?

Winter. I had but come ashore.   What said
he, Leonard?

Vicary. First, he would have the admiral
take the bread ;
Then, when in turn the priest did come to
him,
He said, I would another man than you
Were here to give me of this bread of God.
Yet, as for this dear body of my Lord,
A pearl that 's carried in a robber's pouch
Doth lose no lustre; and with no more words
Took of the sacrament; and so to table.

[*They approach sadly and in silence.*

Doughty. Come, come, I 'll none of this!
Here are bent brows;
You go not thus to battle.   Shall one death

Disturb our appetites and spoil our mirth?

Am I not host?   They 'll not be bid again

Who come not merry. (*Aside to Vicary.*) See
      you fail me not.

Some men ask prayers.   I only ask a smile.

(*Aloud.*) Come, gentlemen, I put this hardship
      on you.

There might be many questions, much to say.

    Drake.   I shall sit here forever, if you will,

But talk I cannot.

    Doughty.   Nay, but that is strange.

'T is the glad privilege of the gentle born

To see in death an honest creditor,

That any day may ask the debt of life.

What! must I make the talk?   That 's naughty
      manners.

I never was a happier man than now.

There 's few among you shall have choice of
      deaths.

And you, Frank Drake? — if God should bid
      elect,

What way to death wouldst choose?

    Drake.   I do not know —

Not in my bed, please God.

    Doughty.   Speak for him, Leonard.

I think my friend has shed his wits to-day.
Once he was readier —

Vicary. Were I Francis Drake,
When waves are wild and fly the bolts of war,
And timbers crash, and decks are bloody red,
Then would I pass, slain by my loving sea,
As died the hurt Greek by a friendly sword.

    Doughty. Full bravely answered. Winter,
      what of you?

    Winter. As God may will. I have no other
      thought.

    Doughty (to Vicary). And what, dear jester,
      Leonard, what of you?

    Vicary. Oh, between kisses, of a morn of
      May,
Or in the merriest moment of a fight,
When blades are out, and the brave Dons stand
      fast —
Upon my soul, I can no more of this,
You ask too much of man. I can no more!
                       [*Leaves the table.*

    Doughty. Now here's a dull companion. Go
      not yet, —
Or go not far, and let not sorrow cheat me.

    Vicary. Oh, I shall smile. Rest you assured
      of that.   [*Moves away.*

Doughty. I thought he had been made of
    sterner stuff.

There's a too gentle jester. (*To Drake.*) Think
    you, Frank,

That we shall meet in heaven?

Drake.   Such is my trust.
                    [*They talk in whispers.*

Doughty (*aloud*). The wind lies fair to
    south. Friends, gentles, all,

It were not well to lose a prospering hour.

God send you kindly gales and gallant ventures!

Strike hard for me, John Winter! When the
    Dons

Are thick about you and the fight goes ill,

Cry, This is for remembrance! This, and this!

And you, dear Leonard, when the feast is gay

Drink double for your friend. Be sure my lips

Shall share with yours the laughter and the cup.
                    [*Rises, as do all.*

Now, then: The Queen and England! (*Drinks.*)
        (*To Drake.*) Take my love.

Still let me live a friendly memory —

Come with me.

Drake.   No, I cannot, cannot come!
                    [*Moves away.*

Doughty (*to* *Vicary*, *as they walk to the*
      block.)   What, not a smile? Not one?
   That 's better, Leonard,
Albeit of a rather sickly sort.
Come hither, Francis Drake. (*Drake ap-*
      proaches.) Good-by, dear friend.
      [*Kisses him on both cheeks. Kneels, and the axe falls.*
Vicary. God rest this soul!
Winter.   Amen!
Drake.   Christ comfort me!